T0132329

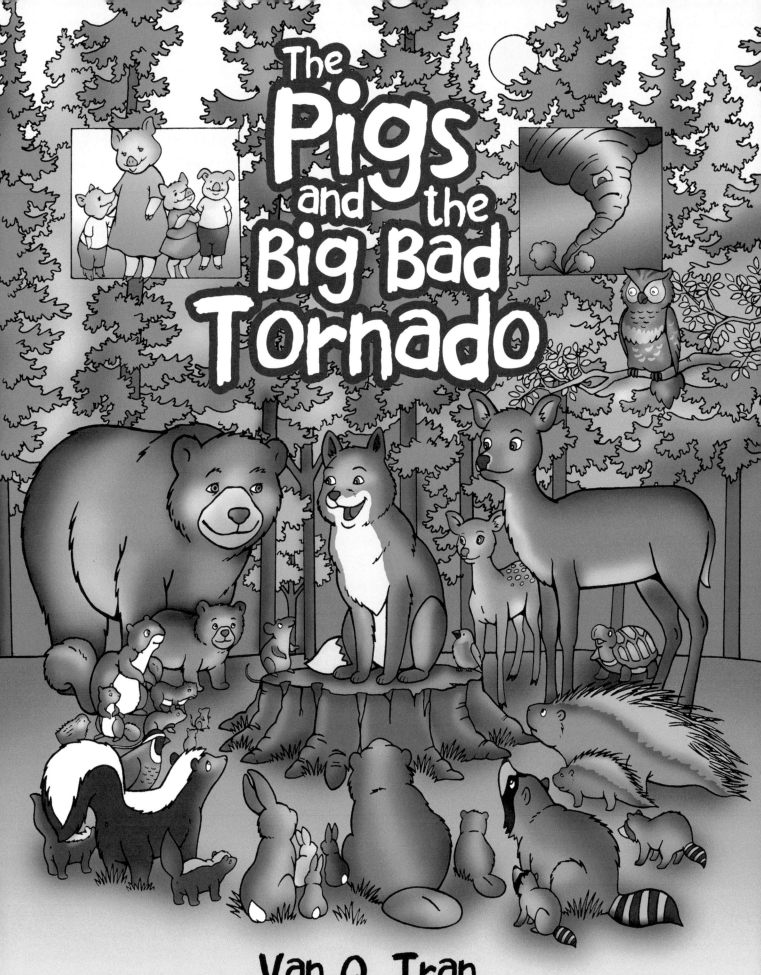

The Pigs and the Big Bad Tornado

Van Q. Tran

AuthorHouse™
1663 Liberty Drive
Bloomington, IN 47403
www.authorhouse.com
Phone: 1 (800) 839-8640

Published by AuthorHouse 04/27/2019

ISBN: 978-1-7283-0934-7 (sc)
ISBN: 978-1-7283-1005-3 (hc)
ISBN: 978-1-7283-0933-0 (e)

Library of Congress Control Number: 2019905196

Print information available on the last page.

authorHOUSE®

The Pigs and the Big Bad Tornado

Along time ago in the forest, a wise
fox told a story-there was a family of
pigs who lived near Tornado Alley.

The mother pig gave birth to triplets. Not long after the three little pigs were born, the big bad tornado came to town; it blew their house and the papa pig away.

The mother pig worked very hard to raise the three little pigs by herself. The three little pigs were born five minutes apart, but the youngest one (Penelope) was not as strong as her brother (Billy) and her sister (Lilly). Since she was a small piglet, she had to work very hard to get her mother's milk to feed on.

While they were growing up, Billy and Lilly just liked to go out to play all day; they were dancing, running, jumping, rolling around in the mud, and sleeping. They did not help their mom with the chores in the house; all they did was eat all the food she cooked.

But Penelope was always around to help her mom with the chores in the house. She helped her mom with cleaning the dirty laundry, taking out the trash, keeping the house tidy, and washing the dishes after meals. She always asked her mom whether she needed any help.

When they went to school, Billy and Lilly did not pay any attention in class or listened to their teachers.

They continued playing, dancing, running, and hanging out with their friends after school. Billy did not want to spend time doing his homework or projects from school. All he wanted to do was to play and sleep in the afternoon. He did not make good enough grades to graduate from high school.

Lilly spent just enough time on her homework and special assignments, but she did not spend any extra time to make sure her work was correct or to improve her assignments. She finished high school, but she didn't want to go to college because there was too much work in college.

Unlike her brother and sister, Penelope was busy helping their mom at home, doing her homework and projects, and even helping her teachers and friends in class. She managed to find extra time to exercise, read books, or see a movie with her good friends. She got good grades and received scholarships from good colleges and universities. Her mom did not have to worry about money to pay for her college.

In the town they lived, there was a big bad tornado that came to town every year. It destroyed houses, lives, businesses, barns, and it took people's livestock away. Its roar sounded like a freight train. It twisted and blew away everything it touched. The piggies were afraid of the big bad tornado when they were growing up because they knew it had taken away their house and their father.

They all promised to find a way to beat the big bad tornado. But Billy was too lazy to care about his promise when he built his house. He collected woods and straws from the forest and fields nearby to build his house.

Lilly spent a little bit more effort to gather plywood at an abandoned woodyard nearby to build her house. It took a little bit longer to build, and it was a little bit sturdier than her big brother's.

Penelope, with her promises in mind, worked very hard through college to study architecture. She also spent time and effort studying the power of the big bad tornado. She earned a lot of money from her job as an architect after college. She was able to design and build her house out of strong bricks, concrete, and iron. The house was shaped like a pyramid, half buried underneath the ground with a safe room inside.

Penelope had learned that the pyramids had withstood the harshest weather for thousands of years. It took a lot of time and hard work to dig in the ground, stack the bricks, pour the concrete, and weld the iron. She built extra rooms in her house so that her mother could come to live with her, where it would be safer; she could also take care of her mother during her old age.

One day, late in the afternoon, the sky turned dark and greenish, with dark clouds approaching. There was no rain, but large hail fell down from the sky. Suddenly, the air grew very still. Then everyone heard a loud roaring sound, like a freight train was approaching. The wind started to twist, turn, and blow with powerful gusts. It blew everything in its way when it came near.

The big bad tornado had not even come close to Billy's house, but all the straws and woods of his house had flown away. He woke up just in time to look up at the tornado's big angry eye in the sky. He got frightened and ran to Lilly's house.

But his sister's plywood house started to crumble as the big bad tornado came near. Both piggies trembled and then got out just in time as the house collapsed; all the plywood was carried away by the wind. They both ran to the youngest piggy's house.

Penelope let them in and took them to the safe room, where their mother was sitting inside. To calm her siblings down, she gave them food and water that she had stored in the room for an emergency. All the pigs listened to the emergency radio for the news about the big bad tornado, and Penelope was reading her book by a lantern to pass the time.

The big bad tornado came close and started to blow at Penelope's house. It twisted, huffed, puffed, and blew, but it had no effect on her house. The big bad tornado got mad and came closer. It twisted, huffed, puffed, and blew harder, but there was still no damage to the house. The tornado got angrier, and it tried harder. But the more it twisted, huffed, puffed, and blew, the more exhausted it got. Then the tornado got a cold when it touched the ground and lost its strength. The dense, towering vertical clouds above its eye started to break up. The big bad tornado faded away and disappeared in the sky.

Billy and Lilly were still shaking from the big bad tornado. They promised their mother that they would work hard to build better and stronger houses, liked the youngest piggy's house. They came out the safe room and checked the house for damage, but the big bad tornado was no match for Penelope's hard work and determination to keep her family safe.

The big bad tornado had left just in time for the piggies to help Mom prepare for dinner. However, this time Billy and Lilly also helped with cooking and cleaning instead of playing around and sleeping.

The smallest little piggy had grown up to become a strong, smart young lady. Through her hard work, determination, and effort, Penelope was able to keep her promise to keep her family safe. She built the strongest and safest house in town; it had defeated the big bad tornado, and she saved her family from its destruction.

Printed in the United States
By Bookmasters